Goodbye, School

By **Tonya Lippert, PhD, LCSW**

Illustrated by **Tracy Bishop**

Magination Press • Washington, DC • American Psychological Association

To my beloved children, Roan and Frances—*TL*

For Courtney, Diandra, Blythe, and Laura–my best book sisters—*TB*

Magination Press

Books for Kids From the
American Psychological Association
maginationpress.org

Magination Press is a registered trademark of the American Psychological Association.
Order books here: maginationpress.org or 1-800-374-2721

Book design by Gwen Grafft
Printed by Sonic Media Solutions, Inc., Medford, NY

Library of Congress Cataloging-in-Publication Data
Names: Lippert, Tonya K., author. | Bishop, Tracy, illustrator.
Title: Goodbye, school / by Tonya Lippert, PhD, LCSW ; illustrated by Tracy Bishop.
Description: Washington, DC : Magination Press, [2019] | "American
    Psychological Association." | Summary: Franny takes her time saying
    goodbye to the only school she has ever attended, remembering everything
    that has made it special.
Identifiers: LCCN 2018027286| ISBN 9781433830297 (hardcover) |
    ISBN 1433830299 (hardcover)
Subjects: | CYAC: Farewells—Fiction. | Schools—Fiction.
Classification: LCC PZ7.1.L567 Goo 2019 | DDC [E]—dc23
LC record available at https://lccn.loc.gov/2018027286

Manufactured in the United States of America
10 9 8 7 6 5 4 3 2 1

"Hello, stairs."
Franny noticed her friendship bracelet folded over on the top step.
She'd lost it the other day. "Hello there, bracelet."

The door of the classroom stood before her.
The whole building was hushed. School had ended,
but no one told her to hurry up or said, "Time to go."

But today, it was time to go.
Franny had to say goodbye.

Franny put her hand on the outside wall of the classroom. "It's okay. It's okay." She flew her fingers over its rough and smooth spots and felt its warmth.

Franny wondered how she could say her last goodbye to her school.

She played here,
read here, learned here,
and even used to nap here.
She had friends here.

Now she was going
somewhere else.

Franny opened the door.
The classroom felt big and small at the same time.

She found her chair that let her see
through the window. "Hello, chair."
Whichever way she sat, the chair held
her. Even the time Billy had tried to
pull her off it, the chair fell with her.
She traced its scratches.

A bird rested at the window.
"Hello, bird," Franny whispered.

She'd miss the window. Every day, she had
watched at three o'clock for all the parents.

Franny breathed. Books. Chalk. School.
Graham crackers.

For a moment, the classroom seemed to have lights and
warmth as Franny remembered sitting with graham
crackers and milk. She felt she belonged. She felt lighter.

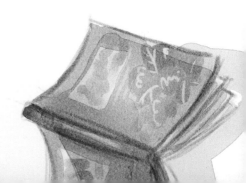

A low shush of wind blew through the
trees outside, making them seem lighter, too.

Franny and her best friend Katie had been friends with the trees. Sometimes, they liked to sit under them and look for four-leaf clovers as the sun and shade slipped across their faces.

Franny knew how
she wanted to say goodbye.

Visiting her empty cubby, she said,
"Thank you," kissed a clover, and set it down.

Franny paused at the table with the green, red, pink,
orange, brown, blue, and faded yellow construction paper.
Orange was always her favorite.

Back at the door, Franny admired her work.

"Goodbye," she said to her school,
solid and strong. Franny pulled her
shoulders back to be solid and strong, too.

Franny hugged her teacher and then her old tree friend.
"Be my classroom's friend now."

Mom asked,
"Are you ready?"

Franny looked at her bracelet and…
one more thing she'd kept.

"I'm ready."

Reader's Note

All children experience changes and transitions—moving, changing schools, a friend leaving town. These changes can bring uncertainty and sadness about what a child may "lose," such as friends, caregivers, teachers, comforting rituals. This is common even when there's excitement about what may be next. *Goodbye, School* is about Franny finding a way to say goodbye when she has to leave a cherished place, her classroom. Reading this book to children who face a change or transition can encourage them to identify and express the feelings and questions they have about what is happening and what is ahead. It can also open up ideas about how to act on their feelings, the way Franny acts on the love she has for her classroom. Transitions and changes can then become times where we recognize how much we care about someone or something. When we feel a sense of loss, it's because we care.

Changes and transitions are not disconnected starts and stops from everyday life; they are bridges between the past and the future. You can help children carry a sense of wholeness and continuity through the impermanent landscapes of their lives.

Below are a few guidelines and examples of what you can say to a child experiencing a change or transition. You'll want to adjust what you say and how you say it according to a child's developmental level and what you know about your child. Also, children often need repetition and may want to have the discussion more than once. Your child may repeat it to you, as they try to strengthen their understanding of what is happening.

Acknowledge the transition.

Acknowledge the change or transition and the feelings that often come with it. For example, you might say, "You are going to have a different school (home, class, etc.) now. People can feel a lot of different ways when something like this happens. Some kids feel sad, some scared, and some mad. Some might feel excited about some of the things that will be different."

Express and validate feelings.

Ask about your child's feelings. Sometimes, children will only tell you something if you ask. You could ask, "How do you feel about going to a different school?" or "How do you feel about your friend moving away?"

Children may express their feelings directly or indirectly. They may cry. They may want to avoid the discussion. Either way, allow and accept the feelings and let children know their feelings make sense. Listen without expressing judgment about their feelings and without telling them what they should feel.

If a child expresses feelings directly, saying they are sad and/or mad, you might say, "Yeah, sometimes I also feel that way when things change but I want them to stay the same." If the child nods or otherwise shows that you've hit the mark, you might go further and recognize how hard it can be to accept what's out of our control. For example, you might add something along the lines of, "Sometimes I wish I had magic powers to make things be the way I want them."

If a child expresses feelings indirectly, try to see what these feelings are or may be. For example, if a child puts their head down, you might try, "You seem sad." If you get no response and the child seems open to talking, you can check your perception with, "Are you sad?"

Validate your child's feelings and guide them toward expressing them in a healthy manner. Let your child know it's normal to have more than one feeling at the same time, including sadness, anger, fear, excitement, and happiness. There may even be guilt. Avoid the temptation to distract children from their feelings or to focus excessively

on the "bright side." Let them experience the loss. Connect the experience to the fact that they care. Tell your child that caring means someone or something was special and important to them and that, by caring, they keep what they love and have loved with them.

Say goodbye.

Assist your child with identifying a meaningful way to say goodbye to someone or something beloved. There are rituals that others have used as well as ones that your child can create, like how Franny used clovers to signify special moments in her classroom. Give them examples and model healthy ways of saying goodbye. For instance, you might say: "I wonder if there's a way to say goodbye to your school that shows how much you care about it?" or "How can you show your friend that you're really going to miss him?" Ask what they think or what they want to do. You may also ask your child whether they want help coming up with ideas, and here is where you can share goodbye or transition rituals that you or others have found useful in similar situations. The point is to guide them toward finding meaningful ways to honor connections they've had and keep them open to building future ones.

If a child becomes stuck and appears unable to attend to other areas of life for an extended period, then you may want to seek counseling. Most children, however, will find that expression and validation of their feelings, and saying goodbye, frees them to move forward.

...ie Author

...ippert, PhD, LCSW, has studied developmental psychology and clinical social work. ...vas a visiting professor at Reed College and worked at Oregon Social Learning Center. ...e currently works at Kaiser Permanente, running mental health therapy groups for ...dults and interviewing children and teens for a medical evaluation of abuse. She also co-authored a book on ADHD. She currently calls Portland, Oregon home. Visit her @tlipk or tonyalippert.blog.

About the Illustrator

Tracy Bishop is an illustrator of more than 20 picture and chapter books. She grew up on a U.S. Army base in Japan and has always loved drawing. Tracy has a degree in graphic design with a focus on illustration and animation from San Jose State University. She currently lives in San Jose, California. Visit tracybishop.com and @tracybishopart on Instagram and Twitter.

About Magination Press

Magination Press is an imprint of the American Psychological Association, the largest scientific and professional organization representing psychologists in the United States and the largest association of psychologists worldwide. Visit maginationpress.org.